VIKING KESTREL
Viking Penguin Inc., 40 West 23rd Street
New York, New York 10010, U.S.A.
Penguin Books Canada Limited, 2801 John Street
Markham, Ontario, Canada L3R 1B4

First published in 1989 by Viking Penguin Inc.
Published simultaneously in Canada
Set in Sabon.
Printed and bound in Italy
Created and Produced by Sadie Fields Productions Ltd,
8, Pembridge Studios, 27A Pembridge Villas, London W11 3EP

1   2   3   4   5   93   92   91   90   89

Waiting My Turn

Karen Erickson and Maureen Roffey

Viking Kestrel

It's hard to sit and wait.

When I'm hungry I want to eat.

When I'm ready I want to go.

But Grandma says "Be patient."

She says everyone has to learn
patience.

Okay. I'll try to.
But what is patience?

Patience is waiting
when you'd like to go.

Patience is sitting still
when you'd like to run around.

Patience is knowing your food will come, but smiling and talking until it does, even though you are hungry.

Patience is waiting your turn.

Patience is playing your
baby sister's game even though
you'd rather play your own.

Look.
I can be patient when I have to be.
I can do it.
I did it.